D1410741

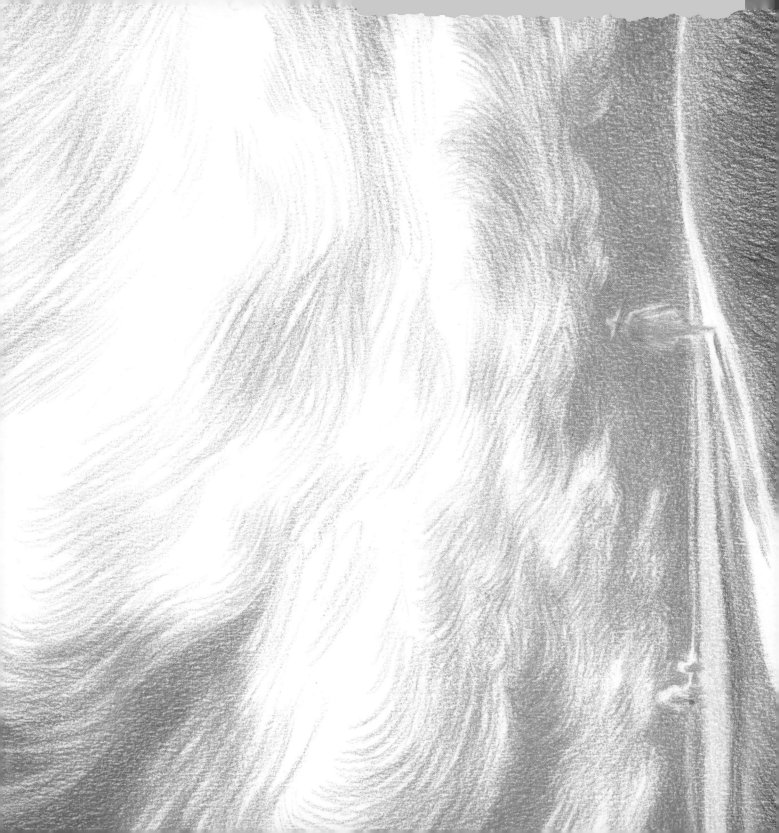

To my three wonderful grandchildren,
Hanna, Arjent, and Emerina.
BDG

To Cristina, Elena, and Lara.
ESG

Green
Bean
Books

FSC
MIX
Paper from
responsible sources
FSC® C005748
www.fsc.org

This edition first published in the UK in 2021 by Green Bean Books • c/o Pen & Sword Books Ltd • 47 Church Street, Barnsley, South Yorkshire, S70 2AS
www.greenbeanbooks.com • Text © Barbara Diamond Goldin, 2021 • Illustrations © Eva Sánchez Gómez, 2021 • Copyright © Green Bean Books, 2021
This adaptation of the classic fable by I. L. Peretz, written by Barbara Diamond Goldin, was first published by the Penguin Group in 1993. This updated edition, with
new illustrations by Eva Sánchez Gómez, was published by Green Bean Books in 2021. • Hardback edition: 978-1-78438-665-8 • Harold Grinspoon Foundation
edition: 978-1-78438-669-6 • The right of Barbara Diamond Goldin to be identified as the Author of this work has been asserted by her in accordance with the
Copyright, Designs and Patents Act 1988. All rights reserved. No part of this book may be reproduced, transmitted, broadcast or stored in an information retrieval
system in any form or by any means, graphic, electronic or mechanical, including photocopying, taping and recording, without prior written permission from the
Publisher. • Art direction and design by Tina García • Edited by Kate Baker • Production by Hugh Allan
Printed in China by Imago • 032134.3K2/B0606/A7

The
MAGICIAN'S
VISIT

Based on a story by **I. L. Peretz**

Adapted by **Barbara Diamond Goldin** | Illustrated by **Eva Sánchez Gómez**

It was the busy days before Passover, and people were cleaning and washing, shopping and cooking. They would have walked by any other magician, violin player, or jokester. But they could not help noticing this one.

He was a wonder. A man dressed in rags, who could pull yards and yards of fancy ribbons from his mouth. A slim figure who found turkeys as big as bears in his boots. He didn't have enough pennies to pay the innkeeper, but he could tap his shoe and produce rivers of gold coins.

The townspeople crowded around the magician.
"Where did you come from?" they asked.
"From Paris."
"Where are you going?"
"To London."
"How did you get here?"
"I wandered here," the magician answered one last time. Then he vanished as if the earth had swallowed him, only to reappear on the other side of the marketplace.

In this very same town lived a poor couple, Jonah and Rebecca.
Jonah had once been a wealthy lumberman, but, through misfortune,
he had become penniless. Now, he and Rebecca had no money to
buy the matzah, candles, wine, and food for the Seder.

Jonah would not borrow money. "God will come to our aid," he said.

They gave what few pennies they had to the Passover fund, for they
were very charitable people. "There are others with less than we have,"
said Rebecca.

On Passover eve, Jonah walked home from the synagogue. In all the windows of the houses he passed, candles glowed on the tables and glasses of wine sparkled before each place. Only *his* house was dark. But he did not feel discouraged.

When Jonah entered his house, he called,
"Chag Sameach, Rebecca!"
"Chag Sameach," she replied sadly.
"Don't you know what day this is?" he asked her.
"We celebrate our freedom today. No tears. If God has
not chosen to let us have our own Seder, then we will
go to a neighbor's. Every door is open on Passover.
Come, put on your shawl."

At that moment, someone called out, "Chag Sameach!"
"Chag Sameach to you," Rebecca and Jonah replied,
though they could not see the stranger's face in the dark.
"I would like to be a guest at your Seder."
"I'm sorry," said Jonah, "but we have no Seder."
"There is no need to worry. I have brought the
Seder with me," said the visitor.

"But we can't have the Seder in the dark," blurted out Rebecca.
"Certainly not," said the visitor. Suddenly, there was a sound like
the snapping of fingers, and two golden candlesticks with glowing
candles danced in the air. In their light, Rebecca and Jonah saw the
face of the stranger – it was the magician!

While they stared in wonder and fear, the magician turned to the table and said, "Come here and be spread with fine linen."

As soon as the magician spoke, the table danced to the middle of the room, and a snowy white tablecloth dropped from the ceiling to cover it. The candlesticks landed safely on the cloth.

"Now we need couches," said
the magician. And three chairs
sailed through the air to three sides
of the table.

"Grow wider," said the magician. They grew
wider, into large armchairs.
"Grow softer," he said. And they were padded with red
velvet. Pillows floated from the ceiling onto the chairs.

Another command, and a Seder plate with bitter herbs, shank bone, greens, egg, and haroset appeared on the table. Matzah, glasses of wine, and all the things needed for the feast followed.

"Do you have water for the washing?" asked the magician. "If not, I can arrange for that, too."

On hearing his question, Rebecca and Jonah came to life.

"Can we touch these things?" Rebecca whispered to her husband.

"I don't know," Jonah replied.

"You'd better go ask the rabbi," she said.

"Let's both go," said Jonah.

Leaving the magician alone with the feast, the two set off to see the rabbi. The rabbi listened carefully to Jonah and Rebecca as they told their story.

"What a magician produces is a deception, an illusion," the rabbi said. "If you can crumble the matzah and pour the wine, if the pillows are soft to the touch, then you will know this is all a gift from heaven."

Rebecca and Jonah returned to their house. Everything was as they had left it, except the magician was gone.

They touched the matzah. It crumbled. They tipped the wine pitcher. The wine poured. They sat on the velvet chairs and sighed. So soft.

They understood then. Their Passover feast was a gift from heaven, brought by the prophet Elijah himself.

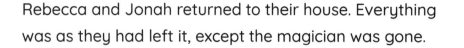

ABOUT THIS BOOK

▶ **What is Passover? What is a Seder?**

The eight-day spring holiday of Passover celebrates the Israelites' exodus from ancient Egypt. Under Moses' leadership, they left slavery to journey toward the Promised Land. Jews have relived the Israelites' journey for centuries by taking part in a special ceremony called a Seder, which is held on the first two nights of the holiday. These evenings are filled with rituals, blessings, singing, storytelling, and a festive meal.

▶ **What do the special foods mean?**

At the Seder meal, certain foods on the table are symbols of the Passover story. Matzah is the flat, unleavened bread the Israelites ate on the night they left Egypt in a hurry. Bitter herbs remind us of the bitterness of slavery. Fresh greens and the roasted egg are symbols of springtime. The mixture of fruits, nuts, and wine, called *haroset*, is a symbol of the bricks and mortar our ancestors used to build Pharaoh's cities. And the roasted shank bone reminds us of the lamb the Israelites sacrificed on the night they left Egypt. Vegetarians often have a roasted beet instead of the shank bone.

▶ **Who was Elijah?**

The Elijah of the Bible lived in ancient Israel around the 9th century BCE and taught about the One God. According to the Biblical book Kings II, Elijah didn't die, but was carried to heaven in a chariot of fire. During the centuries that followed, stories were told about how Elijah reappeared on Earth to help the poor and teach scholars. Elijah became a folk hero and a symbol of hope for Jews all over the world.

▶ **Is Elijah important in the Seder?**

The prophet Elijah plays an important part in the Seder. A full cup of wine is placed on the table for him. Later on, during the Seder, the door is opened, and Elijah is invited in with the hope that his arrival will bring the age of peace.

GLOSSARY

▶ **Who was I. L. Peretz?**
The famous Yiddish writer,
I. L. Peretz, lived in Poland from
1852 to 1915. In 1904, he wrote
the story *The Magician*, which
is rooted in the folk tradition of
Elijah tales. His writings, which
include short stories, poems, plays,
essays, and memoirs, are rich in
the details of Eastern European
life. He was one of the first Jewish
writers to collect and retell Yiddish
folk tales and love songs. He was
also one of the first to be inspired
by the teachings of the early
Hasidic masters. This version of
The Magician is a retelling of his
story for today's families.

Hasidism is a religious
movement founded by
the Baal Shem Tov in the
18th century in Eastern
Europe. Its emphasis is on
devotion in prayer and
the importance of joy and
a feeling of closeness to
God in worship.

Moses was a leader,
prophet, and lawgiver
around the 13th century
BCE. He guided the
Israelites out of slavery
in Egypt and led them
through the desert for
the next forty years.
Traditionally, it is said
that the Oral Law was
given to Moses on the top
of Mount Sinai in Egypt.
He died just before the
Israelites entered the Land
of Israel.

Seder refers to the
special dinner held on the
first two nights of Passover.
The word means "order"
and refers to the specific
order of the ceremony.

Yiddish is a language
that originated in the
10th century in the Rhine
region of Germany. It
was used by Eastern and
Central European Jews for
about 1,000 years and is
still spoken in some places.
The basic vocabulary of
Yiddish is German, with
words from Hebrew and
other languages mixed in.
It's written with Hebrew
letters. Some Yiddish
words and phrases have
been adopted into English,
such as bagel, *spiel* (a tale),
and *oy vey* (oh no!).